In

the

Bank

of

Beautiful

Sins

ALSO BY ROBERT WRIGLEY

The Sinking of Clay City
Moon in a Mason Jar
What My Father Believed

Poems by

ROBERT WRIGLEY

PENGUIN

POETS

In the

Bank

of

Beautiful

Sins

PENGUIN BOOKS
Published by the Penguin Group
Penguin Books USA Inc., 375 Hudson Street, New York, New York 10014, U.S.A.
Penguin Books Ltd, 27 Wrights Lane, London W8 5TZ, England
Penguin Books Australia Ltd, Ringwood, Victoria, Australia
Penguin Books Canada Ltd, 10 Alcorn Avenue,
Toronto, Ontario, Canada M4V 3B2
Penguin Books (N.Z.) Ltd, 182–190 Wairau Road,
Auckland 10, New Zealand

Penguin Books Ltd, Registered Offices:
Harmondsworth, Middlesex, England

First published in Penguin Books 1995

10 9 8 7 6 5 4 3 2 1

Page xi constitutes an extension of this copyright page.

LIBRARY OF CONGRESS CATALOGING IN PUBLICATION DATA
Wrigley, Robert, 1951–
    In the bank of beautiful sins: poems/by Robert Wrigley.
        p.   cm. — (Penguin poets)
    ISBN 0 14 05.8716 0
    I. Title.
    PS3573.R58I5   1994
        811'.54—dc20   94–19923

Printed in the United States of America
Set in Centaur
Designed by Katy Riegel

for Kim

Contents

Three: The Nothing-God

Four: Speed of Light

Acknowledgments

Some of these poems first appeared in the following periodicals: *CutBank:* "A Cappella," "Cigarettes," "Winter Love"; *The Georgia Review:* "Angels," "The Bramble," "The Model"; *The Gettysburg Review:* "Parents," "Seeing the Lynx Again"; *The Indiana Review:* "The New World"; *Kinesis:* "Majestic"; *Manoa:* "Habitat," "Lucky," "Meadowlark," "Spontaneous"; *The New England Review:* "About Language," "Poetry"; *The Ohio Poetry Review:* "IGA," "Plath"; *Poetry:* "Creel," "To Work" (under the title "Homage"), "Little Deaths"; *Poetry Northwest:* "Aubade," "Benton's Persephone," "Hal's Bells," "The Longing of Eagles," "Speed of Light"; *Shenandoah:* "Two Horses, Two Men," "So Long, Sailor"; *The Talking River Review:* "Ornithos."

"Parents" also appeared in *The Pushcart Prize XVII: Best of the Small Presses, 1992–93*, Bill Henderson, editor (Wainscott, NY: Pushcart Press). "Winter Love" also appeared in *The Last Best Place: A Montana Anthology*, William Kittredge and Annick Smith, editors (Helena: Montana State Historical Society Press, 1988).

Special thanks to Kim Barnes, Claire Davis, Dennis Held, and Robert Coker Johnson, who helped in the making of this book more than I can say.

"Let me guide myself with the blue, forked torch of a flower
down the dark and darker stairs, where blue is darkened
    on blueness
down the way Persephone goes, just now, in the first-frosted
    September,
to the sightless realm where darkness is married to dark"
                                        —D. H. Lawrence

"His bones are full of the sin of his youth,
which shall lie down with him in the dust."
                                        —Job, 20:11

PART ONE

Believing Owl, Saying Owl

AUBADE

Sun-baked all day, the south-facing cliffs
breathe fire. The canyon air itself
can't sleep, sheets beneath them
gone incrementally to musk, and the man
at last awakened alone, a train whistle
moaning upriver. Maybe the train's
clank and ratchet brought her out first,
or the hope some breeze has happened,
not fire and water, the river's ice, a clammy flank of air.
Whatever it was, now the moonlight's made of her
a woman burnished by silver, leaned against the porch rail
and looking at the water through the almost-dark.
It's me, he says from the doorway,
and she doesn't turn, but opens
her stance, so that he might kneel
and crane his neck, and lick
along and up the sweet, salt seam
to her spine, her shoulders, her neck,
his hands a fingery wind along her arms,
down the fine column of ribs to the palm-fitted handles
her pelvic bones afford—
                          Lord, he prays, if I have sworn
my loathing for the sun and cursed the salt
that blinds my eyes at work; if I have not slept
but have believed hell a canyon of basalt
a cold clear river taunts through; if I have turned,
scalded by this skin and the murk of damp bedding,
then wake me, wake me by whatever light is called for,
so I might find her, bathed
in a glow that is pure hell alone,
but tempered by her silver
to a dark the mouths remember, breathing
flesh into flames. Let us be candles

melted to a single wax. Let us be tangled at dawn
and lick awake the lids of each other's salty eyes
and rise—

     to welcome the daily fire.

The only word for it, his white Lincoln's arc
from the crown of the downriver road
and the splash it bellied in the water.
Two other passersby and I waded out and pulled him
from the half-sunk wreck, the high collar
of his vestments torn away for breathing,
a rosary knotted in his left hand.
It's an endless wait for an ambulance
there, that serpentine road between distant towns,
night coming on, August, the rocks we laid him on
still fired by the sun. And so we came
to know one another, three living men
touching tenderly the dead one's body,
tending mouth and chest, making
a pillow for the head. He did not look,
we understood, like any man of God.
It was Roy, the mill-hand from Orofino,
who saw the tattoo first—no cross at all
but Christ Himself hung out, crucified
to the pale, hairless flesh by needles of India ink.
Jim, the prison guard, had seen it all in his time,
and looked up sweaty from the breath-kissed face
only long enough to say "Keep pumping."
I cupped my hands behind the doughy neck
to hold the airway straight and knew
as the others knew there was no point at all
for him in what we did. After a while
we just stopped, and Jim began to talk about time
and distance, the site of the nearest phone,
the speed of the first car he'd sent there.
Roy lit a cigarette, traced the flights of nighthawks,
and I waded back out to the Lincoln,
in the open driver's door

a little eddied lake of papers and butts,
where the river lapped the deep blue dash,
a sodden Bible and a vial of pills.
There was something we should say
for him, we must all have been sure,
for later on, when the lights came in sight
around the last downriver corner,
we gathered again at the body
and took one another's hands,
bowed, our eyes closed,
and said each in his turn
what we thought might be a prayer.
Something huge sliced through the air then,
but no one looked up,
believing owl, saying owl,
and at last opening our eyes
just as the day's final light ripened purple
and the black basalt we knelt on disappeared.
In that one moment, that second
of uncertainty, nothing shone
but the cold flesh of the priest,
and on the breast, almost throbbing
with the out-rushing dark—
the looming, hand-sized tattoo of Jesus
we could just as suddenly not see.
Bless the owl then, for passing
over once more and returning to us
the breathable air, the new, unspectacular night,
and the world itself, trailing beneath its talons,
still hanging on and making its bleats
and whimpers, before the noise
and the night above the river
swallowed it all.

THE NEW WORLD

Twelve-year-old hermit, I'd hacked my way alone
into the hillside above the pond, the great oaks
and elms brooding so dark the sun barely shone
on the fortress I'd made. My two daily smokes
I took in the air, out of the earth-bermed shelter,
up the trunk nailed by board, rung, and lath,
in the swaying nest of a crotch. I felt her
there first from that dizzy height, come for her bath,
on the small dirt shore undressing. She hung her shirt
from a stob, draped her pants on a limb,
and dove in. Because I didn't dare move, the hurt
in my legs tingled upward like fire. I couldn't rub them,
I couldn't kick. I could only note
the sway of her breasts midair, how they swung
out as she stooped to dive, their roll and float
when she turned to swim on her back. Young
men and boys dream so often, the skin
of possibility is as common as air, and this woman
I knew as our nearest distant neighbor, kin
of my father's churchgoing friends,
this woman rose in the shallows until I could not breathe—
breasts, hips, dark bed of hair—
and I knew with what sure grinning ease
my father's god could send me plummeting into air.
Dead then from the dull feet upward,
draped numb in the oak's suicidal branches,
I might have called out, or cried, or said a word
I couldn't know; I might have taken my chances
with her rage, just to kick my legs awake,
to save myself from falling; I might have, if the other
woman had not just then appeared, to take
the swimmer's hands in her own and cover
them with kisses. The sky darkening toward night

is a long fall through touch and laughter,
through the sun going down and the last light
high among leaves and sparrows, on me, after
all that time aloft and unmoving, nearly grown
inside the oak's evening sway. What did I learn there?
What did I tell myself when they'd gone
and I'd swung my bristling, bloodless legs in the air
enough to scramble down, weak-kneed
and dizzy in the dusk, into what had always been,
but into a world I felt new in, freed,
where nothing is nothing, and love is a sin.

ANGELS

Cigarettes pilfered two at a time
from her mother's purse, slender black candles
flickering all around us, dripping
a translucent, silver wax. Her father's
favorite records, Brubeck and Baker,
sailing out the French doors,
over the patio and the pool;
her father's gold razor
sliding over my toes, to the arch of each
foot, to the ankle, to the knee and beyond.
The skin of my legs tingled.
Over the fine bone china bowl,
filled now with hair and foamy water,
angels presided, a chain of them
tangled wing to wing
around the rim—in the too pale light,
in the artist's rendering—neither male
nor female but beautiful still.
We'd grunted the old cheval mirror
across the room to the bed,
and I could see her from both sides,
breasts and buttocks as she knelt
to kiss from my legs little ruby after ruby
of blood. A wedding portrait
hung above us, and two slabbed, mug-shot smiles
peered from the nightstands—mother here,
father there, his glasses by the clock,
her night-mask in the drawer.
We didn't speak, we didn't need to:
the negotiations of young flesh,
this for that, mine for yours—one more coin
in the bank of beautiful sins.
I could have had anything

I wanted, and I wanted it all,
whoever I was, that peeled boy
so naked there was no skin
between me and the girl, there was nothing,
so that what I remember most
is the hour just after we stopped,
when she eased back down my legs to kneel
at my feet and hold my heels in her palm,
until nail by nail she was finished,
her lips kissing the air, her breath
coming cool to dry the polish,
an icy burn blown upward through my bones.
She rolled me over and lay down on me
until we slept. I woke
in the dark, to burnt wicks smoking
all around and a dream falling away
as I stretched, the weight on my back
only wings.

SPONTANEOUS

And then one day music only mourned, the sax
blackened in his breath and hands,
an acid in him beautifully burning.
Behind a dark podium, the bouncer wept
for his children, waitresses stalled between tables.
Soon the patrons themselves grew silent,
every drink shimmered in the lights,
a translucent bruise. True, the rhythm section blustered
up-tempo past ballads, drummer gunning rim-shots,
bass man driving toward a stride,
but still the tables emptied—couples first,
disaffected halves lingering in the shadows—
until only singles remained, scattered
each in his own cone of candlelight.
This was an angel they could see,
one more celebrant of sadness, and at the bar
a man who believed in the needle's cure,
and the tenor ready at last to try, for nothing else
could rid him of the vision he was dying by:
not the music, not the horn gone
gray as a pistol, not the woman herself,
come back for the spectacle of his dark immolation,
her left hand pressed against her belly,
her right on the arm of a man who grinned,
and who once, during the music, threw back his head
and seemed to laugh, though no one in the place
would have heard.

CIGARETTES

in memory of Sara Vogan

All the science notwithstanding, it's still
a little like a kiss to me,
or what a kiss might lead to.
That first grand expulsion
of breath from the lungs hangs there
like metaphor given skin,
and we almost believe in ourselves
some new way. Now and then
I bum one, and the rush
of dizziness that results
turns me woman in memory.
Though I lived in the world,
I hardly stepped outside myself at all,
and women seemed a miracle of confidence.
Once I crossed the street
to retrieve the still-smoldering butt
a high-heeled, tight-skirted woman had tossed away.
I touched the lipstick-tainted end to my lips,
drew, and the fire burned my fingers,
the fire she'd taken into herself and sent out
into the air around us like a spell.
The first woman who ever let me
touch her, a girl really, only seventeen,
kissed me so deeply I fell out of myself
and became her. In the moonlit backseat
I knelt upward and beheld my own eyes
in a body of perfection as vulnerable as a child's.
Quick-witted and foul-mouthed
ordinarily, she was silent now,
even as the moments stretched out toward pain,
even when I reached over the front seat

and took one of her cigarettes and lit it
for myself. When she moved at last
it was both arms rising toward me,
and absurdly, I handed her the smoke.
Maybe some tatter of cloud passed
before the moon just then
and in that moment her hands ceased
imploring and began simply to accept.
Whoever we would be for the next twenty years
took residence behind our eyes.
With both hands she eased away the cigarette,
and the drag she pulled into herself
cast a light that left me blind.

THE LONGING OF EAGLES

No words can tell what they feel, how
mated for life they breed once a year
and no one calls it love, what preening
they do in the last light at dusk,
done for the good of the next—pure, habitual,
the sweet uncomplicated essence of instinct.
No gestures pass between them, no eloquent eye
belies a hunger not born of bad fishing,
and the annual surviving offspring blinks once
at its dead nestmate, kicked over the edge and gone.

I do not envy their flights, not climb
or dive or the hover in a hard wind,
outrigger wings gone quiveringly tense.
I do not envy what we call their play,
the swoops and feints, the talons-locked
free-fall tumble in the sun of a false spring.
I do not envy their beauty, nor the keen eye
of the ornithologist, who can tell them apart.
I do not envy the air they fly through,
nor the waters that sustain them,
nor the darkness that has made of them
something rare. I do not envy their dignity.

For two weeks now I watched a single eagle
troll the canyon, and this morning
I found its mate, talons and tail-feathers removed,
a filthy hulk. I do not know if it is male or female,
but I would bet every word I love, the shot
that felled it was fired by a man. I wonder,
as he bent to his work—the hard jerks
at the feathers, the unsheathed
hatchet for the legs—I wonder

if the eyes were open, if even in death
they glared out with that fierce
dispassionate stare of the raptor,
the predator, knowing many things,
but not hatred, not need, not human love.

BENTON'S PERSEPHONE

Autumn, harvest, the pond still clear of dust,
and the mower in the distance shaving the fields
into sheaves. Nothing about her body
is less than perfect. He wants to breathe her,
she was made for his mouth.

Nothing about the wild grape matters,
nor the basket of columbine, nor the oak
he himself resembles, gnarled and nobby,
a few leaves tonguing the air above her
and his hand just inches

from her hip. The distances they've covered:
every year she walks the fields
and sheds her dress of wine, to wait.
Every year it is harder for him
to read the look in her eyes.

Where does such power come from as abides
in that gaze, all languor, the air itself
wet and hot, the blue sky like a lover.
True, when at last he touches her
she'll turn, open, a gift

he trembles to receive. But for now
there is only this moment stretching out
as far as he can feel, as far as she can see,
the awful purgatorial round of the seasons,
through which she never ages

and he never dies, the luxury of lying
untouched, the curse of desire.
Were they not already gone from the fields

and prairies, wolves would howl now.
The moon would tell them

this stillness cannot be. The air would cleave,
the knees of the oak she nestles between
would quiver, and he would gather her up
and bear her home, into the smoke and flame
he bargained for.

THE BRAMBLE

Cathedral of thorns, brambly fist—
how do the snakes get along such thoroughfares,
that deep, spiny mind with no thought
other than swallowing the world.
My arms are crosshatched with scratches
and purpled by juice, my back flayed
like a flagellant's, but I'm not stopping.
The jars I filled with berries look bloody
in the distance—peck of bruised hearts,
glass vat of gizzard and lung,
easy picking at the thicket's edge.
Now I know what the sparrows whisper,
those little breathy drums, damning and damning.
It's a car, old and black. Some odd blink
of sun shone off a shard of glass
and drew me on. I went to the barn
for machete and shears, for heavy gloves and a hat,
and now this shadowy corridor, this hallway of hooks,
this ramp of knives onto soil unwalked
in years. It bleeds pure black under my boot.

Packard or Pierce-Arrow, high-classed and funereal
in its prime, yards off and under
the canopy of canes and berries
nectar-dulled to a plush, velvet sheen.
The light itself is stained glass, the grille darned
with threads of thorn, spoked wheels sewn
to the ground like buttons.
Outside, a raven caws to celebrate the sun,
and the cane that falls before me cries,
or I do, falling back in a fire of spines
at the skull in the driver's window.
What god or devil puts my eye outside me now,

beholding myself caught and wriggling,
and the skull lolling over me—
one fat cane shot obscenely from its mouth,
another looped through an eye socket
and the third, smaller hole in the forehead.
Blood on my right arm, my ear sliced
clean as a mushroom, the first salt drops
purling down the stains on my shoulders—
I stop. Hush, hush, go the sparrows;
the raven still caws. Far away,
a truck's jake blats for a curve.
I loosen myself, one ragged limb at a time, and stand.

Five minutes, a few more cut canes, and I can see
there are two of them, two bodies skinned
by years and the bones inhabited by berries.
I would have thought, over time
some animal big as me or bigger
would have bulled in for such bones,
but now the light comes low, colored by sunset,
the canes red as tendons. I can see
they were man and woman once:
among the visceral thorns, the thoracic brambles,
a gold brooch and a tie tack almost touching,
having grown together over the years, or having died that way.

The porch bell's ringing. Supper's nearly done.
I'll bet my wife stands there a moment, shading her eyes,
wondering where I've gone to, maybe shaking a rag
off the leeward rail, waiting for berries.
Hush, hush, go the sparrows. The light is almost gone,
and I cannot move for thinking, and can't unmake
a tunnel out of light into light,
a door some wandering boy will enter
hunting for snakes, happy for the blackest berries.
But I try, making a weave
from the dead and the living, the severed canes

and canes unending, blood knot and brain weave,
while the bell from the porch goes mad at my absence.
I'm working now on pain alone.
Darkness comes down like a skin
to hide all wounds and bowers—
the graverobber's black suit, the lovers' abandon—
and if I make enough noise, half-bathing
in the horse trough, she'll hear
and drop whatever implement she holds
at the sight of me—slashed and bloody
in the doorway, my right hand
white and unscathed, holding out to her
a brooch of diamonds.

PART TWO

A

Cappella

ANYTHING THE RIVER GIVES

Basalt, granite, tourmaline, the male wash
of off-white seed from an elderberry,
the fly's-eye, pincushion nubbins yellow
balsamroot extrudes from hot spring soil,
confetti of eggshell on a shelf of stone.
Here's a flotilla of beaver-peeled branches,
a cottonwood mile the shade of your skin.
Every day I bring some small offering
from my morning walk along the river:
something steel, blackened amber with rust,
an odd pin or bushing shed by the train
or torqued loose from the track, a mashed penny,
the muddy bulge of snowmelt current.
I lie headlong on a bed of rocks,
dip my cheek in the shallows,
and see the water mid-channel three feet
above my eyes. Overhead the swallows
loop for hornets, stinkbugs, black flies and bees,
gone grass shows a snakeskin shed last summer.
The year's first flowers are always yellow,
dogtooth violet dangling downcast and small.
Here is fennel, witches' broom, and bunchgrass,
an ancient horseshoe nailed to a cottonwood
and halfway swallowed in its punky flesh.
Here is an agate polished over years,
a few bones picked clean and gnawed by mice.
Here is every breautiful rock I've seen
in my life, here is my breath still singing
from a reedy flute, here is the river
telling my blood your name without end.
Take the sky and wear it, take the moon's skid
over waves, that monthly jewel.
If there are wounds in this world no love heals,

then the things I haul up—feather and bone,
tonnage of stone and the pale green trumpets
of stump lichens—are ounce by ounce
a weight to counterbalance your doubts.
In another month there won't be room left
on the windowsills and cluttered shelves,
and still you'll see me, standing before you,
presenting some husk or rusty souvenir,
anything the river gives, and I believe
you will love.

CREEL

for Greg Pape

We sentimentalize the weaver, the hands
that love and bind methodical and true,
wicker tightly wound on ribs. Fronds
of fern too, and rainbow trout blue
and gold and rose, are likewise woven,
fishermen looping the air with their lines.
What is weaving but a kind of love
for what holds: the tines
of branches locked among leaves, sure
elegance of burlap on the bundled roots
of a transplanted sapling, and if you're
fishing, that dark nest at your hip boots'
top, nestled variegations of trout
and leaf, ribs and whitely layered flesh—
streams falling all ways down and out,
the cold fabric of the river, a mesh.

ORNITHOS

Autumn, the hummingbirds gone,
and all but a single, elderly osprey.
A few rube goldfinches linger, boorish,
and the redtails, a local pair
cruising the hillsides for easy pickings;
yesterday a peregrine falcon, folding
and falling, one long plunge past us,
headed south. True,
the gamebirds stay home:
goldeneyes and mud ducks dive
the pools for smolts, processionals of geese
lording over the grouse and pheasants,
little head-bobs a birdy genuflection.
I love the turkey vultures, apocalyptically stalled
on a thermal and watching the highway unwind.
Cawing, custodial, the ravens prosper,
husband the pheasant chicks
that magpies don't unhatch.

Last winter, a bald eagle lifted
into a wet, slanting snow. I thought he saw
a trout, hungry and lolling, nosing the shallows,
but it was a goldeneye,
paddling absently round a pool.
It might change you in the heart you most believe in,
the way the eagle rode that snowy wind
not ten feet above the surface,
making now and then a desultory snatch
with his talons, his call driven off
and the goldeneye diving down until it drowned.

That afternoon a boy found it, draped
across a fat, comfortable branch,

bill yawed open, body cavity neatly cleaned.
I would be that boy if I could.
I would take off my gloves
and lift the snow to my face
like a mirror, hardly scarlet
but pinked, flushed by the cold.
I would call to Raven
to eat and sing with me, those eyes
the eagle's hooked beak abjured, pure
gold, little eggs of light—
O Raven, Raven, sing with me, show me
the darkness I might live by.

FIELD BURNING: A FULL MOON

Cold air comes down like a dome
above the burning fields.
For days the rabbits and mice have fled,
the sky all smoke and rapturous wings.
It is something to see, all right,
cars from town parked along the barrows,
bird-watchers clutching binoculars,
and parents on their knees
tracing an eagle's plummet toward a vole.

Now the moon, a salmon medallion,
some red-faced farm boy leering past a banjo.
Who doesn't love the black birds
coming priestly through the just-cooled ash
and euthanized stubble? They will eat
even cooked meat, they will primp
and call, little tramps of darkness
keeping funereal hours, cassocked wings
behind their backs, furrow to furrow, collecting souls.

A CAPPELLA

for Marnie Bullock

Sensitive fellow and bellower of brimstone,
our two preachers warred
until the younger—married, soft-spoken—suffered
what the congregation called "a nervous breakdown."
We mulled this over and knew
a line had been drawn. Benny left
for the Methodists, flushed with liberalism and luck.
Mark muled off with his homely sister,
Sunday school and two church services per week,
a lost soul sure to sell insurance.
So there I was, child of equal time,
compromise-kid, left to face the abyss alone,
the rib-rattling, stentorian doom
of the right Reverend Mr. Christian J. Kuhlman.
But I could sing, so worked undercover, robed,
a godly doo-wop a cappella spy
dreaming of revenge.
                              How I found it,
slim trapdoor in the furnace room closet,
I don't remember, but shinnied up through
every Sunday for a month to squat
among the organ's pipes, doxologically drunk
and reeling with the heart-rattling air.
Through lattice I could see the congregation
chewing their gristly hymns, heads
bobbing in the battle with sleep.
I could see the righteous and the wretched,
the plump girl I'd talked out of her blouse
in the sacristy, the boy who would die
in five more years, in a jungle
the rest of us had yet to learn.

———

And so it is the way with spring, old
Dionysian horniness afflicting the lewd
and lonely alike: *This is your seed!*
the Reverend Kuhlman roared
to the catechismal boys, who knew better
than to giggle, but half-believed
the church filled up on Easter
for the bulbs of gladiolus, gratis and fraught
with the mysteries of fertility.
We made our glum procession,
junior choir in robes of angelic white.
Christ was risen again, one thousand
nine hundred, sixty-six times—
an avalanche of rolled-away stones,
a gangland, machine gun massacre of nail holes—
but we sang "Today! Today!" a cappella,
from the steps below the altar
while the Reverend Kuhlman beamed
for the seeds we'd become.

After the singing, the procession back out,
most of the choir hung around the flowery foyer,
where crates of bulbs sat like arks,
but not me, easing off, sprinting around the building,
my robe and stifling suit coat flung in the bushes.
I leapt down through the basement door,
the furnace room, and up the trapdoor hole
to the place of held breaths, the forest of pipes.
All the while he raged through a sermon
on sacrifice, I sacrificed my one white shirt
and plucked up pipes and switched their holes,
untuning an instrument seventy-five years old,
stuffing a pile of rags in the heavy basses,
sweating, wild to be back in time
and beaming, my hand held out,
hearty, hilarious, smug as the saved.

———

Lucious Hart, the organist, went apoplectic
at the first chord. I slid back
in time to see him, aging, kindly,
effeminate, fluttering down the stairs
behind the altar, his undone black robe
arcing out like insufficient wings.
And if I guessed the Reverend Kuhlman
would blame the Jews or the Catholics,
it was an honest mistake, the Crucifixion,
cards, whiskey, and the Communist Party
all blamed on them before.
But he didn't say a word, only stood
at the pulpit, his head to one side,
chin slightly up. He looked like Jesus,
shaved and beatific, neither bellowing nor braying
but waiting, until the wave of chatter
washed against the church's back wall
and returned as silence, then waiting a moment more
before closing his eyes and singing of God,
from whom all blessings flowed,
in our church, almost a lament.

So we sang, and for a moment
even those of us who had vowed
never to give in, gave in
to so many ordinary voices trying
to make up for fiasco, to believe in real wings, to sing.
Through all the handshakes after, the hugs and mugs
of aunts and great-aunts and grandmothers,
no one noted the smudge of coal dust on my cheek.
I was, after all, almost a child, dirt magnet,
dog tailed, my voice barely lower than soprano.
The Reverend Kuhlman's hand on my face
was a tenderness I might have known him by.
"Your gift," he said to me, "is music,"
and there was Aunt Betty, snapping our picture,
the one so many years on the wall,

then in the album, for years spoken of
humorously, then ironically, then worse.
It was the day—Easter it was!—
when the Reverend took back his earlier prophecy.
No, he said, I wouldn't preach after all,
but would find another way to make my peace
with music.

HAL'S BELLS

There's a horde of ringer washers
catching an agitated rain, a Quonset hut
upholstered in hubcaps. The long revenge of grass
has swallowed a thresher, and rust
unravels a double rank of Ramblers.
Out back the woodstoves graze
with the cattle, wind across the flues
makes a sad, demented bawling.
And here's a barn full of signs—
the bowling alleys of indifference, the cafés
of rats—one stall aslant with cast-off crosses,
the hayloft congregated by hymnals and pews.
In the house, on shelves nailed
between studs, insulation and drywall
a pink-and-white heap beneath the oak,
every bell you can imagine: prizefight, cow,
door, and church, in brass and steel,
in pewter and tin, in iron, aluminum, bronze.
Every stretch of floor and table, strung
wall to wall on wires everywhere you look,
bells, bells, and old Hal Bell himself, damned
near deaf, grinning as you go
room to room, making the air itself
clang with light.

ABOUT LANGUAGE

for Jordan

Damn the rain anyway, she says,
three years old, a hand planted on her hip,
and another held up and out
in the mimic of a gesture she knows too well—
adult exasperation, peevish, wild-eyed, and dangerous.
But the mangy stuffed bunny belies it all,
dangling by an ear, a lumpy flourish.

And so again I am warned about langauge,
my wife having just entered the room
aims a will-you-never-learn look my way
and I'm counting myself lucky. She missed me,
hands to the window, imploring the world,
Jesus Christ, will you look at the fucking rain!

And because this is western Oregon, and the rain
blows endlessly in from the sea, we let her out to play
in the garage, where I peer balefully
into the aged Volvo's gaping maw
and try to force a frozen bolt, that breaks,
my knuckles mashed into the alternator's fins
bejeweling themselves with blood and grease.

And what stops my rail against the Swedes,
my invective against car salesmen, my string
of obscenities concerning the obscenity of money,
is less her softly singing presence there
than my head slamming into the tired, sagging hood.
I'm checking for blood when I feel her touch my leg.

———

What tool is this, Daddy? she's asking,
holding a pliers by the business end. Then
what tool is this? Channel locks. And this?
Standard screwdriver, sparkplug socket,
diagonals, crimper, clamp, ratchet, torque wrench,
deep throw 12-millimeter socket, crescent,
point gauge, black tape, rasp—

but suddenly the rain's slap and spatter
is drowned in the calling of geese,
and I pick her up and rush out, pointing,
headed for the pasture and the clearest view.
And rising from the lake, through rain
and the shambles of late morning fog,

vee after vee of calling Canadas,
ragged at first, then perfect and gray and gone
in the distance. They keep coming and coming,
and pretty soon we're soaked, blinking,
laughing, listening. I tell her they're geese,
they're honking, and she waves and says honk-honk.
She says bye-bye, geese; she says wow; she says Jesus.

LITTLE DEATHS

Every minute or two, another moth
blunders through the candle flame—a dusty puff,
then silence. Some fall
sealed in wax, others spin
half-charred across the table.
By the handful every hour
I toss them in the stove.

How easy it is to live with
little deaths—mostly bugs,
the less musical birds, the cats
and rabbits we can't avoid in our cars.
My son poked the broken grasshopper
until it almost flew again, then laughed
and crawled after, singing *doot again, doot again.*

In the woods behind their summer camp
Pentacostal kids crucified frogs
to the trees. Three nails
and a sapling trunk, little fish-belly
amphibious Jesus. Once
I shot a turtle, green lump under duckweed,
thumb-nubbin head. I couldn't believe all the bubbles.

There's no accounting for this,
though I fear salvation
is an enterprise, grace the bottom line.
That day last summer, when we lay back
into a cool rocky pool on Potlatch Creek,
we insisted on total immersion,
as though it were a baptism,
as though afterward death were nothing to fear.

———

I have my own ideas about that,
my own cruel sense of who'll die first,
and how. Those four crawdads we caught
were too few for a meal
but perfect fodder for the kids.
The first one, crushed in his rock house,
died by accident, the kids stunned quiet
by the garish yellows, the gray mush inside the carapace.

I'm tempted to say the next two
just expired, suddenly, quietly dead,
though the dog, standing in the washtub
to drink against the heat, may have trampled one.
And the third, when it died,
made a decent meal for the last,
and the last lived weeks and weeks
until we took it to the river.

We stood on the rocks and said good-bye,
then upended the bucket—what was I thinking?—
not in the shallows, but over a deep hole
out of which a huge, shadowy bass
blasted up to take the bait I'd set
for no other reason than catching myself.

Tonight I'm alone at the cabin.
Now and then one of the candle-seared moths
skitters off the table and the dog rouses
and noses it until it's dead.
A few of the livelier ones she's eaten.
Now she sleeps by the stove and sometimes whimpers
and seems to run. I should outlive her by years,
though I think of her dreams and wonder,
whimpering that way, if she is the one who chases.

PART THREE

The

Nothing-

God

SEEING THE LYNX AGAIN

First time it was only the low-slung,
quick-looking, enormous catness of him—
not spotted but mottled, not brown but dun
and driving steadily into the dim
green shade of the next downriver thicket.
Now I follow and find the winter's scat,
flat spirals of feather and fur, dark lick
of the beetle's happy lapping. And that's
the buff clutch of eggs from a pheasant's nest,
spit back to grass and sun, rice-paper dry
but recognizable. Off to the west,
the chickens he won't kill, God knows why.
And God knows some dog will find him one day,
down where Ice House Spring purls from rocks
and the blackberry canes grow thick and gray
as Satan's wrists, there where he sits and mocks
and licks the rabbit's blood from his paws,
where the rattlesnakes sound their alarm.
God damn the dog that will drive him
into the rifle's long eye, so the farm
and its minions may sleep the dumb sleep
of the soon-to-be-robbed, or ridden,
or eaten. Until that day, may he keep
himself out of sight, keep himself hidden
even from me, whose wish is that he stay
here forever, hunched like a housecat,
half-asleep in the wind-scattered shade
under sumac, but eyeing me. He knows
I'm wary of the bottomlands,
where poison ivy oils the air, down below,
where his kittens worry the slender bones
of a chukar some hunter winged the week before.

I'm empty-handed, he knows it, then he turns,
makes a long, yawning stretch, and stands—
suddenly gone, vanished in the ferns.

MEADOWLARK

Something's gotten the neighbors' little dog:
they found it in the brush near the mailbox,
torn, neck-snapped, neatly eviscerated.
We gather to examine the carcass,
then walk home, all but Jeff, wrapping it
in a towel, but maybe thinking of his daughter.
When we're out of earshot, Emil turns,
as I knew he would, and says "Lion."
We'd been talking coyotes, or a bobcat,
but all of us must have known, the dog's head
scrawny, crushed like a ripe plum,
neck snapped by a single hard whip-sine shake.
"Out here," he says, "a dog like that's just bait,"
and I agree. I never liked the thing
anyhow, how it humped my legs and yapped.
But I'm thinking of my son, only three,
how he loves the summer light gone purple
at dusk, how he hides and calls to me
where. It's Sunday morning and the sun's hot
already, one sweet die-hard meadowlark
working his sad, ineffectual key.
"You going to church?" Emil asks, knowing
I'm not. We've had that discussion before.
"Best listen to your own dog," he says.
There's a little charge of current in me now.
He feels it, looks me in the eye and smiles.
Last he heard, his youngest boy was coked out
in the Tenderloin, cross-dressing and bound
for something worse than any easy death.
Hasn't heard from him in more than two years.
"But they all die, them dogs." He's read my mind,
looks hard at me again, then walks on.

"Meadowlark like that one must be crazy,"
he says, and I agree, though we're silent
the rest of the way, alive in that song.

HABITAT

Remnant of last night's storm, the puddle swarms
with cliff swallows this morning,
seethe of flutter on the muddy ground,
orb of glass in the air. It looked
in the slant of the sun
as though the dirt itself were breathing.

Nobody much lives where we live,
the world itself could not care less,
and certainly not the county seat,
miles off and planning bonds
to build another golf course.
I waved and smiled, hollered
"Howdy, neighbors!" and went on my way.
From the bench road, through binoculars,
I could see the swallows still bathed.

Should we pity the poor water-striders
caught propped in that puddle
on their tents of legs? They wouldn't know
swallows eat nothing not in flight,
those kissing squeaks and clear chirps
squawk and skirl over the muddy broth.
Should we celebrate the snake,
a hundred feet aloft in the talons of a hawk?

I saw it out the bedroom window
my head propped on a pillow
as you kissed your way across my chest.
Downstream, the robins in town
bask beneath the rainbird arcs
on public parks and lawns,
and all my life I've wondered why.

In every direction the land pays
out unpaved, and pure water purls
from springs like sweet perfection.

Hath the rain a father? the birds
their fluttery dreams? It's spring.
Even the weeds are joyful
in their darkness, and the bobcat,
having nailed another neighbor's yapping dog,
must likely feel today
he could blink the rifle away
like a gnat and go on sleeping,
the next rank of clouds coming on.

Where we live, the cottonwood fluff
blows up in snowy windrows, and flowers
appear—lupine, syringa, balsamroot, phlox—
taking singular bows and subsiding to green.
Great vees of Canada geese cruise straight
up-canyon at the level of our eyes,
and goldfinches splash from the thickets
like sun-dazzled water. I'm saying
the hawk's hard cry is no god-

like warning. I'm saying the true
single-fingered Idaho wave a neighbor nods
from his pickup cab is something
a coyote could understand. We're blessed.
I'm saying we're blessed, we're blessed,
and take your lovely face
in my hands and bless it,
and point upward, out the window,
so that you too, even now, might see.

WINTER LOVE

from the diary of D.D. Pye (1871–1900)

I

They talked about the cold, the cold
each one felt warm in and believed,
breath clouds so long before their faces
when they spoke—months,
indoors and out—that speech became
unwieldy, frozen, cloud talk
and vapors, a rim of ice
on the lip of the morning blanket.

They made love then, and she rose
and knelt above the chamber pot,
a fog of them rising round her thighs.
He threw back the hides and covers
so his mist in the cabin rafters
might meld and mix with hers.
Love, when they talked, was what
they said. Love, she said,

and he did too, wadding rags in the heaved log
walls, kindling in the swollen,
buckled stove. The wood into flames
unraveling was their music,
and the low reports outside
as trees exploded, frozen to their hearts.
One morning the hens were dead,
in each cloaca, a frost-tufted egg.

2

We know, for all the dead
weight of winter, they never wept
to be back in Pennsylvania, but loved, and lived
on the frozen deer he hauled back
from the snow-locked meadow, one flank
here and there worried by coyote,
hacked away and abandoned.
He never felt watched in the crystalline woods.

Over years now we see the blunder,
the misfortune: a gorgeous homestead
worthless in a trapped-out mountains,
giddy lovers awash in dreams. And winter,
the steel of it driven through their lives,
how it took hold when they touched it—
a kiss of ice in the frozen world
that held them longer than they held each other.

Until the day the fire took the cabin,
when the stove gave way to a last
overload of wood and they huddled
on the tramped-down path to the outhouse,
warmed in a way they had not been
in weeks, until that day the diary we read from,
in his crisp, formal hand, revealed
only joy, and the color of her eyes.

3

The lovers, see them now, those first few
miles in a snow so light it is never
entirely fallen, but a kind of frigid fog
swirling under the useless sun.
At camp that night, in the deep bowl
wind-scoured round a fir tree's butt,

there is terror in his words,
a darkness, malevolent and haunted.

And his love is numbed to stillness
after violent shivers, her breath fitful,
obscured to him by the wind above them
and the rumble of his heart.
He vows to change course. Damn
the distant town and houses. He knows
a spring that boils beyond the western ridgeline,
and if its heat is from hell,

if he must move aside Satan to sit there,
to lower his love in its curing waters,
if he must carry her all the snow-clogged miles,
then so be it, he will. That is all
we can read, but for one entry,
one line without date, one
sentence scrawled dumbly, simply,
as though the cold at last had killed his will.

4

"She is gone." Only that, and the rest
of the story, pieced together by those
who found them, she floating naked
in the steaming waters, he hung from the spar
of a spring-killed tree, diary
beneath his clothes, frozen there,
a flimsy shield across his chest.
Nothing more, but what we imagine:

how the last morning she could not
walk, how piggyback he carried her,
wading through that sea of snow,
feeling against his neck her cheek
foolingly warmed by the touch of him,

the sweat and grunt and ache of how he walked;
his blackened fingers fumbling her
out of her clothes, his scream

at those same fingers when he held her
in the heat of the pool.
How he must have swayed with her
there, light in his arms
and caught already in the slow, unceasing turn
of the current—two lovers
dancing in the hot and buoyant waters,
below the cloud of steam that hides their breath.

THE NOTHING-GOD

Tamarack needles have begun to fall,
a golden snow, hands of a thousand watches.
Another year's unwound and still
the saws in the distance whine like flies.
She lifts her long skirt to feel
the mountain wind, and sees
in the cedar grove across the creek
a blue-and-silver shimmer, beckoning, calling.

When her knees could no longer bear the prayers,
she stopped telling, and one night went down
before the altar, under a spirit
that set the brethren's teeth on edge,
more upright than ever and silent as snow.
That was the first night she lay
tied to the bed, a thin, knotted thong
of hide zinging in her father's hand.

Nothing-god, she whispers, and the light blazes once,
like a sun-shattered mirror, then goes back
to throbbing. The preacher's son has seen it too,
or claims to, pinning her to the kitchen door,
building an evil only he can undo.
And maybe it *is* what brings her visions,
even now she half-sees a whipshaft crown
snapped down the bank to the road

her father walks, the lower bones
of his legs driven through his boot soles,
half a foot deep in the marl and muck.
He dressed her one night in her dead mother's
Sunday clothes and wept to see his own tears
lining the face beneath him, lightning flashes

in the flicker of candles, his greatest fear
the fires of hell he could feel in his eyes.

She's saying her name now, a single up-sung complaint,
like the call of a mournful bird, and when
his truck grinds down the steep trail to the shack,
she'll feel that shimmering fog return to her—
the nothing-god, allowing this world to happen
nightly, again and again, every mark on her
instantly numb, the nothing-god,
the soul of ice, and winter, winter coming on.

HOLLYHOCKS IN NOVEMBER

Eye to eye with the top blossom, I see
a fringe of frost, fading
in the just-up sun or from the nearness of my face,

and the pastel mandala of its middle,
delicate and unstrident, bland
sexual pupil seeing every bee for miles.

Organdy, crepe, the lippy variegations
of the petals; wind-lash, nerve-stalk,
mind of humus, mind of soil, mind of root.

I stand with my last child, crumbling
to the dirt at our feet
the abundant wheels of identical seed.

I G A

I

Meaning to pay, he slips the pack of Camels
in his pocket, and makes his way
toward the counter and the girl. She rings up
the juice and the jelly, the Polident
and the paper towels and says the tab
as he stands there, making her
wait, knowing there's something else,
something else. After all the miles
of this life, his body's a bent hulk
no hag would love a wink from,
let alone this tawny, blue-eyed girl,
her name, Esme Marie, stitched in red script
above her breast. The town whistle sounds
and he looks up, expecting lights.
"It's noon," she says, her voice bored and flat
but promising silver, so he says her name
and smiles, until she repeats the total
and he pays.

2

He's one of those old men
with a ceremonial way of spending money,
pulling the single bill through his fingers
until it's folded in a gradually opening vee
she hardly sees at all. Her free hand
trips the switch that calls the young
assistant manager, the one who last week caught her
sneaking out wine in her purse
and made her pay before she left
and will again until she helps him catch

five more, this old man her first
and her shift just begun, three more days in the week
and not a single other store in town
with openings, not a soul in the lot
but the old man fiddling at a Dodge's locked door
and looking up as the assistant manager
calls out "Hold on."

3

So she knows he's serious now,
though she doesn't look up when he comes
back in, the old man's arm
in his hand, and her back
to him just the clue he needs to see
the way she'll be tonight at closing.
He's thinking last week and looking down,
feeling by rote the turn out of produce,
feeling the peach-soft skin,
when the heavy bottle of juice catches him
square on the bridge of his nose.
He can no longer tell who kneels or why—
to beg or surrender or die—and the very air
around him is swallowed by a tune
everyone in the world must know the words to.
The catchy pyramid of cereals
falls underneath him
and the driven grunts he hears might be hers,
or the old man's, lifting his bottle,
or his own, eye against the picketed lines
on a cereal box bar code.

4

Maybe she hears
a stock boy heaving boxes off a dolly, keeping busy.
She hates the long empty afternoons,

violins sawing the day into slices.
Paper towel and glass polish in her hands,
she peers into the red bottomless divot
of the cash register scanner,
as though it might tell her the dollar
value in her eyes, what it is she must be,
before the cloud a thousand touches made
is wiped away, and she sees.

ULYSSES

There was a shaft of absolute blackness
in him, a depth no dropped stone could plumb,
and her body filled it, the fine,
sweet reciprocal, all-out happy fuck
of lust and yearning, not just cunt and cock,
tongue, lips, and buttocks, but a time inside
the single skin no one can inhabit
for long, enough, or ever. Though they tried,

and, laughing, tallied by their frequency
the tonnage of semen he would leave her
in a lifetime. A day or two later
he went home to his wife and tried to act
like he was trying, and could hardly play
with his son for the absence in his hands,
could not bear to lose the scent of her
at his crotch and would not consent to bathe.

What if love's not love at all, but a way
of blinding the self to its vacancy,
the way *want* is first an absence, a lack,
before it is need, before it's desire?
His wife, you see, wanted him anyway,
everything she said to him the same,
the begging, of course, and then the curse:
that whenever other lips touched his cock,
he'd feel his son's gone arms around his neck.

The nearness of her is oceans away,
though his mouth begins inside her. All in all
it has made him wise to the words of love,
the way one absence can't fill another,

how, across the country of her belly
and breasts, she cries out his name,
while her blood goes on rowing, toward somewhere
he'll never be.

PLATH

Pet dogs of the long dead, coyotes braid a skein
of the purest mourning. Then suddenly,
undetectably, there's playfulness
in their howls, sexual politicking,
some true dog version of the hierarchies
of high opera, arias and old bones.

By candlelight, the cabin windows are gothic,
the rare yews called out along the slopes
blackening in a wind wholly of the mind.
Moments ago another tree gave way
and the wind licked again the bottle's lips.
What, in all this noise, is the night singing?

The wind has a woman's face.
She is dead and now rushes wild around
the world her words cannot stop making.
She is dead, but desperate to wake us
wherever she might be: we must save the children,
we must never look too hard at the sea.

PART FOUR

Speed

of

Light

LUCKY

Here he comes, forlorn and tick-ridden,
skulking down the fencerow
and favoring his right forepaw.
Last year, with a honed linoleum knife,
his owner slit the baby skin
of the scrotum and cut loose his balls
like half-ripe grapes. His sad, misshapen head
locked between the man's knees,
the two sons each holding a hind leg,
it was over in an instant—*snip*,
snip, a splash of peroxide,
and he was on his way,
true model of meekness and loss,
headed for my house.

He's better now, almost cravenly affectionate,
and sometimes breaking into a full run
after Violet, our black Lab bitch,
who even before could sprint away from him
with ease. She's a fine young animal,
and some days they lie together
in the sun, almost preening.
Occasionally he mounts her anyhow
and thrusts and thrusts, instinctive, archetypal,
and driven. She'll be in heat again soon,
and the canyon winds will bring the dogs
for miles—a nervous week
for the cats and chickens,
a tawdry, unsettling display around the kennel.
And Lucky, furtive, suddenly fox-like—
he'll hang back, baring his fangs, calling out,
making his singular complaint, a snarl,

while Violet whimpers and paws at walls of wire
that will not give.

SO LONG, SAILOR

for Keith Browning

Good-byes, good-byes, leave-takings, retirements:
no one can say them all, so long
a list it is. Someone dies, someone is no longer
visiting, a child climbs onto the school bus
that first day, turns on the step to wave,
and opens a wound on his father's heart.
A man leaves his lover for a week
and remembers how his palm slid away from her
breast, how the fingertips lightly followed and held an instant
her nipple. All the time
he is gone, it is as though he invented her,
shaped her, dreamed her warm breath.

Any absence may have its end, and that
is the reason we are living, hope
a dream of reunion, why we believe in waves
miles inland, mountains on the oceanic plains.
Think of the beautiful monotony of the sea,
and of our tiny circumscribed lives on land.
So long is what the ocean says too,
when the sailor embarks on the voyage
to his human lover. Goings and comings,
departures and returns, a regular breathing.
Everything he returns to is just the way he left it
in his dreams—a child's wave, a grave,
a woman's breast—all the world,
the way it fits his stunned, opened hand.

THE MODEL

Last year, too far into my life
for it to matter, I learned how paper folded
into flight—a stubby, nose-heavy plane
that, properly launched, lilted a long ways.
And I was lilting too, a little drunk,
a little nervous for the wind blowing
in from the dark, and honestly frightened
by this tiny, commuter plane—one seat
either side of its stooped, low-ceilinged roof.
Bent over so, I couldn't see the others
already on board, and I was last one on
the nighttime leg to Coeur d'Alene.
How hard I worked, my studied nonchalance,
my legs crossed, and the magazine I pulled
from the seatback, something called *The Model*,
a hundred pages of lean young women
remote as the cold runway below.
I looked, while the twin props blasted the air
and blue lights hurtled off behind us,
at an article about breasts, their care
and maintenance, their myriad shapes
and sizes. Out the window, the city
must have paled and flickered out. Idaho
underneath its clouds hardly shines at all
with light, but with a moon-honed emptiness
strung between its outposts. And I might have
become more than a little interested
in breasts and tight buttocks, in starvation
diets, and limberness I believed
only the slow-boned province of children;
I might have slept, the ride above the clouds
straight and smooth, and the engines' noise a great
white wall of breathing, but the little boy

66

one seat forward and across the aisle
began to misbehave. He went rigid
in his seat and swung out his bony fists
at the young blond woman across from him.
He squealed and shrieked, she fended off punches,
refastened again and again his belt,
and clapped her hand tightly across his mouth.
Up front, beyond a pair of empty seats,
four other children—the oldest about sixteen,
the youngest maybe eight—spoke in sign,
oblivious to the caterwauling
behind them and the whole plane's numbing drone.
I felt a tap on my shoulder
and across more empty seats a man leaned
and spoke to me: "You can come on back here,"
he said, smiling, nodding to the others,
all of them speaking, hearing, refugees
in the ear-shattering world of silence.
But I couldn't, for now the boy took hold
of the empty seat in front of him
and slammed it forward and back, forward
and back, making a loud, guttural cry.
There were groups of us then, little cabals
from the nations of the state of living:
the pilots, swaddled in headsets, consumed
in their lofty work; the deaf children
quietly reading, gesturing their lives
among themselves; the two hearing couples
uneasy in the back, now offended
as well, and in the middle of the plane,
three of us spun together in midair,
a vortex of nothing and the noise between
the walls and the sure enabling wings.
I don't know why I did it, what I thought
it could mean to the wild boy beside me,
but I ripped a page from my magazine
and folded a woman's lovely face down

across her forearm, and brought her perfect,
unimprovable breasts together in a vee and handed
that little boy the only paper plane
I have ever learned to make and fly.
He slung it forward in the cabin, into the lap
of the oldest boy, who grinned and might have
sent it back, had he not seen on one
elegantly folded wing a nipple
shining in the nighttime sky of the plane.
He nudged the boy beside him
but I could not see what they said or did,
for the wild boy alongside me pounded
at my knee, demanding another plane.
This one I made slowly, as he watched,
each crease precise, each angle examined
for symmetry, then unfolded it all
and handed it to him. How easy it was.
He was shocked by the simplicity,
unfolding and refolding it twice
until he was certain he knew. We kept on—
first the two of us, then the young woman
joining in—and soon all that plane
was a litter of crashed and glossy wrecks,
the heartbreaking, uninhibited laughter
of the deaf, of the hearing, hearing again.
When one plane at last made the cockpit
both pilots craned around, moon-eyed.
They could not believe what they saw,
but pulled the curtain closed behind them
and made their long approach to the runway,
the airport, the hard world
about which, I believe, they must suddenly have remembered
nothing but the absolute joy of flight.

TWO HORSES, TWO MEN

The mare shows first, pure shadow
come true out of the last dark
and a ground fog of swimmable wool.
Then the gelding, nervous, not so much skittish
as stupid. *Geld,* my neighbor says, *lobotomize—*
what's the difference? Before
I walked through the orchard, gathering
winesaps and pippins, before I came
to the fence myself and strummed the top strands,
before the horses appeared, I heard him
across the creek as he slid his barn door open,
heard the tractor grind, start, and idle
toward ready. I listened past its noise
for him, some tool clank or smoker's cough to show me
what I already knew he was doing. Then
I heard the horses, and saw them,
saw a rank of crows stepping off
the stubble for bugs, and a lone rooster pheasant
head-down to hear the world come to light.
I'm the outsider recently arrived,
with no job to speak of save this hearing and seeing,
and I swear his joke seems aimed at me, whose morning chore
is apples and a kind of inventory of givens,
as though I might catch the earth
at its secret life—the wandering barn,
the dancing trees whirling off their leaves—
as though I believed more in its magic
than a man whose life is soil and food.
It's still barely light, or mostly dark,
but he's under way. He knows his fields so well
he could cultivate all night long, smoking,
looking now and then at the stars,
now and then at the fog-slicked furrows

behind him, rolling over, lolling open.
But who am I? Fool in the half-light,
out of apples dreaming an earth of wind
and words? I'm nearly nose to nose
with the gelding, who waits and waits,
not noticing my lack of apples, nor the absence
of the mare, well out into the pasture
and nuzzling the newest grasses,
sweet, cold, and sweated with dew.

SPEED OF LIGHT

There's a kind of drunkenness all boys feel
two or three times in their lives. Part laughter,
part light, it can afflict them on playgrounds
long after school has ended, long after
their mothers have called. We see them, turning
in each other's arms the old roughhouse dance
of delirium, when every funny thing
is nothing at all but that which lands
them on their backs, crying the blood's true joy.
Or it begins in boredom, in the night,
the two of them sitting on a curb
below a streetlamp, pounding the half-white
baseball again and again in their mitts.
The first throw upward surprises them,
for though they'd love to shatter such a light,
neither has the nerve to try it, to come
closer and closer each successful miss.
They notice, however, how the baseball
simply vanishes past the light,
then reappears in a dangerous fall
at a spot some distance removed from where
they'd have guessed it. And that is how they are
when their fathers from opposite streetsides
behold them—one on his perfect young arm
rocketing a baseball into darkness,
then both of them poised, alert, heads thrown back,
making every time the startling catch.
From their windows the fathers know it's risk
that drives this game, and maybe something else,
some hopeful way of knowing competence,
the way the crumpled note is a young girl
one dreams of, the wastebasket a sentence
to make love clear at last. It is nothing

they have not lived through, the fathers, and now
they find themselves caught up and believing—
first in the throws, the easy motions, how
the ball stays aloft long enough to live
a life beneath, and their sons, as agile
and quick, as sure-handed as big-leaguers—
when in its dive out of darkness the ball
with a washtub clang hits the light's steel shell
and freezes the sons in an arc flash
before the dark. Now the sobriety
of time, the headache of old memories,
now in their lighted windows the fathers
are visible and must come out and try
to make of it some unforeseeable
thing, not just the same untrustworthy sky
but a hundred glassy shards in the dark,
wastebaskets overflowing with failure,
and a dizzy sweetness falling away
too fast, too fast, as fast as light, faster.

TO WORK

The three-bladed, dunce-capped agitator pulsed,
and steam billowed into the basement rafters.
Monday mornings, in a broth of soap and clothes,
my mother wielded her stick, bleached dun
and blunted with probing, then fed the works
through wringers to a galvanized tub.
Those summers the neighborhood blossomed
with laundry. Sheets snapped and dresses swayed,
a shirt dragged its cuffs through the dandelions.
By early afternoon, by the basket load
lugged in, the laundry stiff with sun was spread
across the kitchen table for sprinkling.
I remember my mother's easy motions,
her thumb mostly over the bottle's hole
and the clothes rolled tight and stacked
like cordwood in the cooler.

And when the light leaned into dusk—
when my father in the gap between his two jobs arrived,
dinner done, dishes washed, my father gone again,
the tiny, round-eyed television squinting
over us—my mother hauled from the hallway closet
the rickety wooden ironing board
and began her final Monday chore.
I sprawled across the rug
and picked at the pills on the hand-me-down sofa,
the whole house filling with the smell of heat
and watery steel, the ironing board's creak,
the iron's dull thunk and glide.
Last thing she pressed was sheets,
one set for each bed in the house,
each bed remade in my sleep

before she lifted me off the floor
and eased me away for the night.

Then the night itself unwrinkling,
new sheets warming into sleep.
That last summer in the old house
many times I woke up late,
my father finally come home and collapsed
in bed alone, while I wandered the halls
to the kitchen, my mother at the table
in a bright wedge of light. I looked up
past the bulb on her sewing machine
at a thicket of pins between her lips.
And in my sleepiness it was one gesture—
her palm across her mouth, a shaken head—
and I was asleep on my feet,
hand in my mother's hand
as she walked me back to bed.
I don't remember ever arriving there,
nor the straightening of the covers,
nor the kiss she might have given me.
I don't remember the house we walked through,
nor the colors of the walls, nor the colors of the clothes
she labored over every night,
the clothes she made for herself,
in which, come September, she would look for work.

IN GRANDMOTHER'S BUICK

1

Her white-gloved Sunday fingers slid once
around the wheel, a charm for all I knew
more necessary than fuel and the fine
and final arrangements of mirror and hat.
Then the quick chime of keys,
a bolt of sun from the single broken window
above the abandoned workbench.
The old straight-eight stuttered alive
and rumbled in our bones like a dream.
What I saw above the dash was sky
and tree, a sudden light
illuminating our legs and the dash
now diamond-studded—radio, ashtray,
the stern faces of the instruments.
My grandmother's arm hung over my shoulder
as she backed slowly down the driveway
and onto Linden Street, where she honked
just once the loud blatting horns
for her husband, my late grandfather,
a habit no stranger than my own,
watching, as she turned the wheel, my face
loom and vanish, loom and vanish
in the chrome ellipse of the horn ring,
that face said to resemble the dead man's
we now bid good-bye to with a single blare,
for whom, every week, we said a prayer.

2

Surely she hated it, the suicide knob,
palm-heft crank on the Buick's wheel:

a nude brunette leering years
across the cab of his truck,
then transferred, a retirement concession
to soften the move to town.
But why, when he died, did she leave it
and learn its hard recoil on corners,
and nestle her white-gloved hand
across the breasts that never changed
regardless of years or miles
or the fingers dreaming them real.
Sunday mornings I'd go out early
and warm the Buick up and ease it
from the narrow garage, and wait.
How many Sundays was it, years of them
looking and looking, until I knew
that body as well as my grandfather
must have known it, knew it all
in a single blaze of Sunday morning light—
then she was tapping at my window,
it was time for church, would I drive,
and I did, as slowly as she would,
my eyes never leaving the road.

PARENTS

Old two-hearted sadness, old blight
in the bones, the history of sugar
and the daily syringe, show tunes,
Shalimar, car after car after car.

Here are my names, all three
trochees ratcheted out like comeuppance,
here my oldest living forebear,
the Depression, my nose, my love for jazz.

Let us locate our first marriages
festering in the cedar closet.
You show me proximity, I'll show you
the blank expansiveness of the West.

O roads, varicose and meandering,
bloody Kansas after Kansas between us—
there are days I'd kneel to kiss
the knuckles most like my own, other days

When a blue Pacific sun shows me all
that's possible, whole oceans of air
I can dream myself a kind of prince in,
a kind of bird, who believes he reigns there.

We're in a new state, and the dandelions
are strange, thin-stemmed and somehow sophisticated-
looking, a kind of botanical, West Coast cool.
But I notice the bees still plunder them,
even on this windless Monday the blossoms bobbing
an undulant syncopation I can't quite ignore.
The babies are asleep, and the heat when I enter you
is some true thing I'm dreaming, not a memory at all
but the body's one life, constant, expansive, simultaneous.

I can hear you putter in the kitchen, domestic these days,
and I admit, what I'm imagining now
requires your body, but not mine, my mind,
but not yours, the counter, the sink, the cloudy light
sliding from your shoulders and over your breasts,
across your belly, a drop of saliva or sweat
silver bauble on a hair and right before my eyes.

This life's already so familiar, I can tell what pot
you hold by its ping against the cabinet door.
I can hear the refrigerator uncatch,
its yawn of light, its full and satisfied hum.
But for some reason the weather's
gone and changed. Now a great flock of crows
rides a thermal out of the trees along the creek,
bees have taken cover, and upstairs
the babies murmur and stir. Dandelions sway
in unison, a decorous, chilly dance.

• • •

Listen, soldiers, I'd sell out the nation
to see my wife come in this room

with my skin on her mind. I'd pledge myself
to Jesus to see the light on her face
I might generate inside her. If she doesn't,
if I don't, it will have nothing to do with art,
or war, or the soul's blind abandon.
It will have nothing to do with weather
or crows, or with dandelions panting away
in the wind, having started all this unawares,
ubiquitous for the bees and their droning, yeoman imperatives:
the seasons, the sun, this great, odd, and unfathomable drive
toward the dark.

ABOUT THE AUTHOR

Born and raised in the Midwest, Robert Wrigley has spent the last twenty years in the Northwest, mostly in Idaho, where he now lives with his wife, Kim Barnes, and their children, at Omega Bend, in the canyon of the Clearwater River. He has received the Frederick Bock Award from *Poetry*, the Celia B. Wagner Award from the Poetry Society of America, two Pushcart Prizes, and two National Endowment for the Arts grants, as well as two fellowships from the Idaho Commission on the Arts. His previous books include *The Sinking of Clay City* (Copper Canyon Press, 1979), *Moon in a Mason Jar* (University of Illinois Press, 1986), and *What My Father Believed* (Illinois, 1991). Educated at Southern Illinois University and the University of Montana, he has taught in the MFA Program for Writers at Warren Wilson College and at the universities of Oregon and Idaho, and he has twice served as Richard Hugo Writer-in-Residence at the University of Montana. He is currently a professor of English and Poet-in-Residence at Lewis-Clark State College, in Lewiston, Idaho.

PENGUIN POETS